Refugees from Eden

Refugees from Eden

Voices of lament, courage and justice

Rosemary Power (Ed.)

wild goose
publications

www.**ionabooks**.com

Contents of book © individual contributors
Compilation © 2021 Rosemary Power

First published 2021 by
Wild Goose Publications
Suite 9, Fairfield
1048 Govan Road, Glasgow G51 4XS, Scotland
the publishing division of the Iona Community.
Scottish Charity No. SC003794. Limited Company Reg. No. SC096243.

ISBN 978-1-84952-785-9

Cover image © jycessay/123RF.com

The publishers gratefully acknowledge the support of the Drummond Trust,
3 Pitt Terrace, Stirling FK8 2EY in producing this book.

Overseas distribution
Australia: Willow Connection Pty Ltd, Unit 4A, 3–9 Kenneth Road,
Manly Vale, NSW 2093
New Zealand: Pleroma, Higginson Street, Otane 4170, Central Hawkes Bay

Printed by Bell & Bain, Thornliebank, Glasgow

'Render a decision.
Make your shadow like night –
  at high noon.
Hide the fugitives,
  do not betray the refugees.
Let the Moabite fugitives stay with you;
  be their shelter from the destroyer.'

Isaiah 16:3a–4 (NIV)

Contents

At the edge of society

Strangers and neighbours

The knowledge that empowers

Blessing

Introduction

The current large-scale movement of refugees across the world is a matter of urgent humanitarian concern. This short book reflects, from a Christian perspective and its requirement for acting justly, on the consequences, especially in Europe and in the United Kingdom. It engages with people the French call *Exilés*: refugees, asylum-seekers, migrants, those who, for whatever reason, have been forced to wander from their own country and culture, and seek support, often temporary, in another land. Here, carrying the scars of their experience they may meet with ignorance, hostility, uncertainty, forcible return, and the kindness of strangers.

We are, all of us, refugees from Eden, whether the journey is spiritual or physical. Many of us yearn for a return there, while others set out in hope of a promised land of safety and new beginnings. Some of the writers here are, or have been, refugees themselves; some have chosen to remain anonymous; and some, because of the impact their experiences have had on them, or because of uncertainty with English, have preferred that their story is told by others. Many of us who are not ourselves refugees are descendants of refugees. Some writers are natives of our continent, who have sought to support through volunteering where displaced people have gathered, or in their own localities, providing hospitality and supportive action. For many this is bound up with the consequences of Brexit and the further tightening of the nation's borders, even as people seek safety by crossing the dangerous waters that divide Britain from France.

Writers include members of, and people in sympathy with, the Iona Community, a Christian organisation with a commitment to the costly peace that arises out of true justice. This book seeks to explore, mainly through the medium of story, how we accept our responsibilities under scripture, international law and human morality to provide sanctuary to those fleeing violence and persecution. Written in the hope that each of us can provide ground for our politicians to seek new ways of addressing the forced movements of people around our world, the authors offer their reflections to inspire, support and encourage others as they seek the strength of Eden, *'the goodness at the heart of humanity, planted more deeply than all that is wrong'* (from an Iona Community affirmation).

We start with lament, grieving the departed, and our part in the loss; then move to the wider world situation; then to Europe and to the U.K. As we see, most who come to our shores are eager to contribute to the common good, whether their stay is temporary or long-term.

This book is dedicated to the memory of all who have undertaken the perilous journey from their homelands, and have not lived. Their bodies may lie unclaimed in sand or sea, and we have lost potential medics, climate scientists, carers, parents and grandparents, and much more. A society is valued for how it treats its least-known members, and we cannot forget those lives cut short through desperation and when fellow-humans let them down. As refugees from Eden, wanderers, committed to providing hospitality as Sarah and Abraham once did, we are required to deal rightly with the stranger in our midst. Further, we are bound to seek Christ in the face of each person, the Christ forced as an infant into exile.

Rosemary Power

Prologue: Lament

Requiem

Re - qui - em ae - ter - nam do - na e - is,

re - qui - em ae - ter - nam do - na e - is,

Do - mi - ne, Do - mi - ne,

et lux per - pe - tu - a lu - ce - at e - is.

Requiem

Requiem aeternam dona eis,
requiem aeternam dona eis,
Domine, Domine,
et lux perpetua luceat eis.

Eternal rest give unto them,
eternal rest give unto them,
Lord, Lord,
and light perpetual shine upon them.

Words: traditional

Music by Charles Hulin

Dè cho fada, a Thighearna?/How long, O Lord?

Dè cho fada, a Thighearna, dè cho fada?

Shìos, shìos fon talamh
tha fuil Abel a' glaodhaich,
a' chiad neach a dh'fhuiling murt:

Dè cho fada, a Thighearna, dè cho fada?

A-mach anns an fhàsach
tha Hagar a' caoidh
ann an èiginn a trèigsinn:

Dè cho fada, a Thighearna, dè cho fada?

Tha màthraichean na h-Èiphit
fo bhròn an ciad-ghin
a' gearan mu raige Phàraoh:

Dè cho fada, a Thighearna, dè cho fada?

Thig mac-talla bho Bhetlehem,
Raonaid a' caoidh a cloinne,
ciad mhartairean an Tighearna Ìosa Crìosd:

Dè cho fada, a Thighearna, dè cho fada?

Coltach ri boladh geur,
cuiridh iad an glaodhaich ris
an fheadhainn a dh'èireas fon altair nèamhaidh:

Dè cho fada, a Thighearna, dè cho fada?

How long, O Lord, how long?

From under the earth
the blood of Abel yells,
victim of the first murder:

How long, O Lord, how long?

Out of the desert
Hagar cries out
in the anguish of her abandonment:

How long, O Lord, how long?

The mothers of Egypt
mourning their first-born
protest the stubbornness of Pharaoh:

How long, O Lord, how long?

An echo comes from Bethlehem,
Rachel crying for her children,
first martyrs of the Lord Jesus Christ:

How long, O Lord, how long?

Like a pungent aroma,
they mix their voices with
those which scream from beneath the heavenly altar:

How long, O Lord, how long?

Rory MacLeod

Beyond our shores

Yad Vashem

*In considering the current international crisis, we might go back to the origins
of our 1951 Refugee Convention, on which subsequent legislation is theoreti-
cally built. The vilification of certain groups in the Nazi period, most particularly the Jews, and the consequent attempt to murder a nation, lies behind the
creation of laws that remind us that never again should those fleeing persecution be turned away.*

*Outside the World Holocaust Remembrance Center, Yad Vashem in Jerusalem,
a large outdoor sculpture by Nandor Glid, a Holocaust survivor, commem-
orates the Jewish dead. (Ed.)*

We did not find you
in the bazaar
on the Way of the Cross
so we bought bright baubles
and carried carved camels.
Our ersatz experience
cost thirty pieces.

    Then we came to a place
    where skeletal forms
    stretched starkly under a livid sky.
    Backs arched
    in one continual agony
    over the twisted iron limbs;
    fingers spread like giant thorns
    pushing us away;
    skulls screamed silently
    accusing us

who were not there when it happened –
or were we?

It was this –
this metal monument of death
which pierced our apathy
and brought us back to life again.
We shed our tears then, burning
with shame and grief.

    And we found you there –
      weeping with us.

Margaret Connor

Conversations I can't forget

I

We're drinking coffee on a suburban stoep.
'I've got this great kid in my class,' she says.
'You know what a rough school it is. And he really stands out.
I noticed a pattern: he was absent one Thursday a month.
So eventually I asked him:
"What is it that keeps you away from school one Thursday a month?"
I thought maybe he had to go to a hospital
for some sort of treatment or something.
"I sell drugs," he said.
Well, I nearly fell over! And he's such a good kid.
I couldn't speak. Not that drugs are unheard of at that school. But him!

"The money pays for school fees for me and my brother. And rent.
We are from Mozambique.
We ran away".'
He didn't mention desperation, fear, grief, hunger, loss.
He didn't mention that they must have waded or swum across
the Limpopo, the Limpopo with all its crocodiles.
He didn't mention that they must have walked through the Kruger,
the Kruger with all its lions.
He offered no excuses.
'He trusts me,' she says, 'but now I have this information.
What should I do?'

It's years later and I still don't know the answer.

II

We're working alongside each other in an artists' printing studio.
He works there every day. I come once a week.
He's young and talented and black.
I'm having my little rant about corruption and he listens politely.
'We simply mustn't pay bribes,' I say.
'If a cop catches me speeding I must simply pay the fine.
If I want my water problem sorted I must stand in the queue.
No bribes!'
He steps back from the table and gazes at me as if amazed.
'Are you saying that never in your life have you ever paid a bribe?'
'Yes', I say.
'You're so lucky,' he says, very slowly and very seriously.
It is then that I remember that he is Mozambican.
And I remember that I am indeed lucky.

Holding the moral high ground is an economic privilege.

III

We're on a rural school campus in Zimbabwe.
I'm visiting for a week.
'Sue, who are those men I hear calling to each other in the night?
And what's that clinking of tools?'
'Oh, it's the illegal miners,' she says.
'They're reworking the old dumps. Panning in the river.
When they've got a big enough lump of gold they put it in their pockets,
nice and portable, and try to cross the Limpopo to South Africa.
They pay bribes all the way.
What's left if they reach so-called safety is easily changed into cash.'

Elizabeth Davison

Notes: Although the civil war in Mozambique ended in 1992, there have been no gains for the poor, conflict continues and there are now armed Islamist groups there as well. The South African government grants very few people refugee status, so refugees have to depend on their own ingenuity.

A quarter of the Zimbabwean population has fled Zimbabwe, mostly to South Africa. There are regular reports of refugees drowning in the Limpopo or being eaten by crocodiles. People originally fled because Mugabe's government became increasingly repressive, and this repression continues post-Mugabe. Since South Africa does not officially recognise human rights violations in Zimbabwe, 14,000 Zimbabweans are deported back every week. Small amounts of money are sent home by refugees to help keep their country going.

See
Relief Web: https://reliefweb.int
Human Rights Watch: www.hrw.org

Keep on dancing the samba!

In my early twenties, as a summer job while I was trying to finish my university degree, I taught English as a second language to refugees and asylum-seekers at the YMCA in Canada.

It was an amazing job – I met so many amazing people – from Central and South America, Vietnam, Eastern Europe ... Meeting all those people really opened my eyes – and mind.

I met a family who had taken to sea in a leaky boat with twenty others to escape government troops who had attacked their village.

I met a man who had escaped a prisoner of war camp in Iran, and had walked over mountains and deserts in his bare feet.

I met a woman who had fled the Shining Path in Peru, not long after giving birth to her daughter, whom she carried through jungles and cities on her back.

And I met Marco, who had been a labour leader in a factory in El Salvador, and had been arrested and tortured by the police – he was the most gentle, generous person. It amazed me how someone who had been tortured could still be so gentle and loving. I certainly wouldn't be. I guessed he understood something about the fragility and preciousness of life.

I had a certain respect and status as a teacher. Government departments would contact me to enquire the progress of certain students; and some-times I would write letters to colleges and schools for students so that they could get onto training courses. It felt good to be able to help these new friends.

Sometimes we'd all go for coffee after class. One thing that amazed me was how active in Canadian life many of my students already were – in parent groups, tenant organisations, credit unions – and how involved in life back home they remained. They had escaped horrific conditions, yet were in regular contact with not only family and friends but underground groups and organisations working for freedom and justice in their lands. I probably would have just wanted to leave the past behind; keep my head down – for the fates of many of my students were far from decided: some could still be, and likely were, sent back 'home'.

One Christmas, Marco invited me to a party at his community centre after midnight Mass – it was great. There was dancing and live music – a band with conga drums, guitars, a flute, someone playing the marimba. There were fold-up tables crowded with food – roast chicken, rice, potato salad, fruit – cold Mexican beer sweating in a big metal washbasin. The hall was so hot and cooking with music, dancing and conversation I forgot it was twenty below outside. For a moment I forgot I was in Canada. I watched Marco, who had been tortured by death squads, dancing the samba. I watched him expertly move his feet that had been bastinadoed. You can't chain down the human spirit, I thought.

His daughters were full of life. Over the passionate music, Rosanna told me that she wanted to study to be a doctor after high school. Maria said she wanted to be a schoolteacher. Their open smiles radiated spirit, and I thought of how lucky Canada was to have this family as citizens. They seemed hope and new life for a country that seemed to me – cold, hard, stiff, apathetic, individualistic; still white as snow in places. Marco came over and gave me some rum to try. It had a spicy, hot sweet kick. He laughed, and we went out to watch the fireworks. Later, Maria tried to teach me how to dance the samba.

I received Christmas cards from the family for years after. Every Christmas it warmed my heart. In the last one I received, Rosanna was a doctor, and Maria was a nurse and was married – and had just had a baby girl. 'Thanks for being such a great teacher,' Marco wrote. 'And keep on dancing the samba!' he nudged and winked. I could hear his laugh and see his great big smile.

Neil Paynter

Butterfly

I was like a butterfly dancing over the spring flowers.
I was like a breeze caressing the jasmine trees
to reveal their fragrance throughout the place.
I was like a yellow leaf that fell from a branch,
covering the ground with a new colour.
I was like a cloud that blocked the sun,
so that raindrops fell on the thirsty earth, and watered them.
In my country and on the land of my ancestors, the country of Jasmine,
where there is security, safety, goodness and beauty.

We were living the most beautiful moments of our life
and the spring of our days.
But what happened that evening?

A black cloud occupied the middle of the sky,
pouring its anger on the jasmine, burning its perfume,
and turning its pure white into a dark red colour.

The freezing cold attacked the atmosphere of Jasmine
to become the country of death.
Even the butterflies hid in fear and terror in the country of safety,
and the spring flowers migrated,
which withered in sadness for Yasmine Al-Sham.

Our tears fell on that miserable evening to irrigate the wasteland.

We decided to stay, but to leave was the strongest.
So we packed our bags that contained some memories,
a handful of our country's soil,
and a single white jasmine
that had fallen on our balcony before that evening.
We bid farewell to our land and our home
and went out into a new world in search of the security and safety
that we had lost.

We lost a warm hug.
We lost a part of our soul.
We were displaced.
And we became west.

Laila Khaled Alrefai

Note: The Jasmine country is Syria, and its mother, Yasmine Al-Sham, Damascus.

Hearing the silent voice
A conversation for three people

Mary:

In the terror times
the killing fields
came to the House of Bread.

They stabbed the ones he'd toddled with,
eaten with, cried with and dozed in the arms of the parents.

How could those people forgive when
the universe alive in each child
was snapped, cast aside, trampled as worthless.
Was there one soldier that day, paid to slay,
who turned from his orders and passed by in silence to save?

Joseph:

Later I told how we'd fled for our lives,
under the dark; the stark loss and silence
in leaving, saying nothing, fearing all
on the long road through Gaza,
chariots and pickups kicking dust in the face, and us parched,
but afraid of the proffered lifts and drinks and hidden costs,
me powerless to protect:
he'd seen with infant eyes.
All goods we carried were stripped from us,
dignity ripped from us,
in bribes, thefts and inflated prices.

We reached the sea and saw the coast ahead
but no waves parted, though the full boat
foundered on the further shore. We lived.

Border Control voice:

Illegal migrants, asylum shoppers, queue jumpers and other vexatious arrivals will be returned to the country they arrived from. The newly arrived Joseph Jacobson must provide documentation, including proof of residence and occupation from the recent Palestine census, whereabouts of birth and marriage, nationality, and evidence of the alleged danger to life on which the claim for asylum is based. The claim will be processed in due course, and meanwhile the family will be provided with accommodation in a place of our deciding, and a small allowance will be made for basic food. Neither he nor his wife is permitted to work meanwhile, nor to undertake education other than language lessons. Should the claim fail, they will be allowed an appeal but will no longer be eligible for any financial support or accommodation, and will remain ineligible for employment. Should the appeal fail the family will be deported to their home country if deemed safe under current guidelines, and otherwise to a safe 'third country'. The couple can at any stage opt for voluntary repatriation with their child.

Joseph:

It took months too many to count,
dependent on foodbanks,
clothes from the drop-in place,
until they gave us
temporary leave to remain.
I found work, at times.

The Man of Terror died and the powers here decreed
it safe to return. Before they deported us
we left and joined the swarm
to cross the border before
the new regime closed it
against political exiles, criminal gangs, and us.

Mary:

The boy saw this, but saw too the goodness.
He heard from the jeerers who wished us good riddance.
But a border guard muttered 'Courage' and waved us through;
a soldier gave silently his food to a youth;
and the wayside station with water at no cost
offered shoes for our boy, sanitary needs, respect.
A servant gave Joseph the coat that warmed us at night.

We met those heading north, who shared what they had,
the campfire, the food and protection;
those who did not;
and those who charged money at interest.

We taught our boy not to judge
by language, or colour, status or group,
but always each one by themselves.

Joseph:

He saw me carrying the soldier's pack in the heat.
I sensed the quick tense anger for his dad, then his voice
soft, curious, asking the man's story, listening to wandering years
till the stilled thug found his mile complete.
'Your lad'll go far,' he told me.

> We'd always yearned for home.
> But things proved still fragile, not good enough
> to make us go back to where we'd come from.

Border Control voice:

> Report. Exit papers were issued for Mr Joseph Jacobson, his wife
> Miriam and son Joshua. Though members of a minority group that
> we keep under close police observation, and though they attended
> a place of worship which we monitor, neither he nor his wife were
> known to hold views injurious to national security or imperial peace.

Rosemary Power

I took a bus to Bethlehem

I took a bus to Bethlehem.
(Our driver liked the people there.)
We planned to spend some time with them
To show that 'English people care'.

Is this the way to Bethlehem,
By chanting crowds on Jordan banks,
The sad, attenuated stream,
Those burned-out chariots and tanks?

Yet in those pillaged homes and lands,
With frightened guards and suicides,
On quiet minds, with steady hands
The Everlasting Mercy rides.

Godfrey Meynell

At the edge of Europe

You'll die at sea

Abdel Wahab Yousif, from Sudan, was one of 45 people who drowned in the Mediterranean Sea in the autumn of 2020, when their ship was shot at by a group of men and caught fire. Authorities from Libya, Malta and Italy were all called but no one came to their rescue. People are frequently imprisoned, abused, exploited and enslaved in Libya, and yet the EU has a policy to 'push back' to Libya asylum-seekers who are found at sea. One who survived these shipwrecks, saved by local fishermen, said: 'The Europeans let people drown and take them to Libya, because it is easy for them. I can't believe it. I can't believe what happened to us. We drowned and there was fire everywhere! Nobody came! Some ship could have saved us! But no one came. (From the Care4Calais Facebook page)

Abdel Wahab Yousif (1990-2020) wrote this poem shortly before his death.

You'll die at sea.
Your head rocked by the roaring waves,
your body swaying in the water,
like a perforated boat.
In the prime of youth you'll go,
shy of your 30th birthday.
Departing early is not a bad idea;
but it surely is if you die alone,
with no woman calling you to her embrace:
'Let me hold you to my breast,
I have plenty of room.
Let me wash the dirt of misery off your soul.'

Abdel Wahab Yousif, from the Care4Calais website

Refugee
Ezekiel 37:1–3

Darkness is coming, not twilight,
nor the eclipse
but a place in the soul grows silent,
over Europe, overseas.
In places where most live in fear,
our brothers' tales stay unheard.

When he came
across the desert of bones
that will not flesh again;

when he was a slave, like Joseph,
scarred by lost labour,
imprisoned with no stars;

he longed for the land of promise.

He crossed a poisoned sea
in a hungry sunset,
packed in a boat that foundered.

Fishermen drew up skulls, socket-dark,
facing the promised land.

Rosemary Power

The power of the child

'Sbarco!'
As I peg out my washing in the sunny backcourt
I hear the shout go up from my colleague
through in the office
at the front of the blue-and-white-painted house in Via Pirandello.

Mental note:
pull on a T-shirt – pick up the passes to let us onto the dock – pack the PPE;
and we are into the battered silver car,
footwells still glistening with sand
trailed in yesterday from an hour snatched at the Spiaggia dei Conigli.

We speed through the streets of Lampedusa, stopping
only to pick up a nun we know
who brings a lifetime spent in North Africa,
fluent French, Arabic and kindness.

At the dock we spill out of the car,
empty the boot of its pre-packed cargo of water
and, now, masks.

We join those already waiting:
tabarded MSF; T-shirted UNHCR; plainclothes Frontex and police;
behind us, at the gates to the dock, the journalists,
cameras peering through the metal railings,
with a couple of casual onlookers.
One way or another, we've all been called here today.

We wait together,
feeding each other the few scraps of information we have:

two groups expected, one from Libya and the other from Tunisia,
70 nautical miles and a million lifetimes away.
We wait together, and in the distance we see the boats.

The first to arrive, too fast, crashes into the dock.
It is little more than a floating canopy,
packed with young Tunisian men
carrying no luggage but desperation.

They disembark and form a bedraggled line,
their welcome a mask and a temperature check.
We snatch a brief exchange as they take our water
and, without protest, enter the minibus, waiting
to rush them to the sheet-less mattresses of the hotspot.

Minutes later, the second boat, a coastguard vessel,
deposits its exhausted cargo of 26, their boat and its broken engine,
abandoned after four days at sea,
Libya barely behind them.
We watch them
quietly
as, barefoot, they stagger ashore
and then we see the first baby.

Her cry breaks into the tension on the dock and
releases us from our restraint:
frees us all to articulate true concern for the welfare of the weakest,
whatever our role in this strange theatre.

She makes humans of us all.

Fiona Kendall

Notes:

Sbarco – arrival

Hotspot – the initial reception point for refugees on the borders of the European Union

At the foot of Europe's mountains: Bihać, Bosnia

Written about volunteering with an aid organisation

The broken glass crunches underfoot as the rain begins to fall with increased heaviness from the grey sky. The empty windows of the old factory gape blindly down as pairs of eyes and smiling faces follow us around. 'Hello, *salam*, how are you?'

Seven or eight hundred people stay in the old factory on the edge of the modern city of Bihac in Bosnia: on the edge of the city and on the edge of society. The mountains are visible from almost everywhere, as is the terrible scar that marks the Croatian border. Ten kilometres of trees were cleared to better spot those trying to cross, leaving a horrendous eyesore dominating the view. Broken and mismatched shoes tread the filthy ground. Torn and dirty T-shirts fail to cover the bruises and scars of the violence that everyone has faced from the Croatian and Bosnian authorities.

Conversation leads quickly to why we are all here. 'Which country? England is good. Germany is good!' Fleeing war in Afghanistan, persecution in Bangladesh, impossible lives in Pakistan. 'We thought Europe was a better place. Why do they treat us like this? Please, tell your governments what is happening.' Rain begins to pour through the broken roof as we share the truth of the politics with each other. The governments of Europe know, they fund the brutality of the Croatian border authorities. But the people don't – the people need to hear.

The smell of woodsmoke trickles through the cavernous space. Tiny fires between bricks are used to make simple bread, expertly rolled and flattened. 'No, we don't sleep here any more. We sleep in the forest because the police wake us and rob us every night.'

We had gone to talk and to find out the needs of the people here. 'No one else comes here. No one talks to us.' The biggest needs? Food, clothing, medicine, blankets, dignity, liberty, safety, a future.

Hannah Parry

Aziz and Wahid: Best friends in the Balkans

I didn't know then that it wouldn't always rain in Serbia. It had rained for a week without stopping, and bringing hot food to people living in the forest by the border was a challenge. The van had nearly got stuck earlier that day, so we were instead walking beside the train tracks in the dark.

We didn't know then that Aziz and Wahid would become our unlikely friends. Fifteen- and sixteen-year-olds from Afghanistan, they had both been seeking safety and a future for many, many months. Aziz was eleven when his parents sent him to join an older brother in Germany. Three and a half years later, he still hasn't made it. They met us cheerfully in the mud that first night, and we saw them nearly every day during the hot Serbian summer. *'Sababa guru'* we'd say. We would bring dal or rice in takeaway boxes for them to take back to the rest of the group, and sit and chat a while. 'See you tomorrow.'

Aziz told us that there used to be an old factory where they could stay in Šid, the little border town we called home. Living in tents and being unwelcome in the town was a deterioration in conditions that had happened very quickly. They had tried to cross the border into Croatia and the safety of the European Union. Croatia illegally deported them back every time.

'Tomorrow I go to Bosnia,' said Aziz, who was ready to pay 300 euros in order to try from there instead. So we said our goodbyes. But the next day he was still here: there had been a hitch in the plans; and then the day after that we got a call. The police had been to the forest and cleared everything, burnt the sleeping bags and wrecked the tents. After a night of uncertainty, his group had moved to an abandoned house on the edge of the next village. We packed up the food and drove out there. It was raining and dark, we got lost, there were frantic exchanges of messages: 'We're coming – nearly there!' Aziz's grin appeared at the window underneath his big hood. The next day he really was gone. And a day later, we were off to Bosnia too.

We hoped not to see them again until they were settled in Germany. But we got a call from Aziz. His part of the group were pushed back from Croatia and deported to the middle of nowhere. We hurriedly exchanged location details. 'Charge nearly finished. Please. So hungry.'

We found them all, dirty and tired, deep in the mountainous countryside, at the side of the road. The food we brought them was quickly devoured while some injuries were attended to. It is illegal in Bosnia to give a lift to people on the move. They had to walk back to the city – over fifty kilometres.

Two days later we got a similar call: Wahid's part of the group was pushed back too. When we found them, Wahid was particularly injured, his legs covered in sores from the parasites that inhabit the waters in Croatia, and his feet badly blistered from all the miles they had walked.

Aziz and Wahid stayed in the fields around Bihac, where we were working. The boys were stuck whilst extra restrictions were in place due to political posturing preceding a demonstration by a mayoral candidate. They weren't allowed to take the bus back to Sarajevo, despite having bought tickets. The camps there were full anyway, with the city struggling to cope with the number of people on the move, trying to survive. So we met them every day, just like before. We charged powerbanks, brought food and medicine.

Two nights before they left, we brought juice and biscuits to share and sat together on a blanket. Hidden behind my car in some scrubby wasteland at the edge of town, it was a rare opportunity to connect. Helping is criminalised, and even sitting sharing food could be problematic. We revised the Pashto that they had taught us, and looked through the photos we'd taken together. There had been another day in the rain where we'd taken silly selfies, hoods up against the weather. We reminisced about Serbia, the people we knew and where they were now. We managed to name each person: Helen's back in London now; Riaz made it to Italy; Sheersha is in France … We went through each face and where they are now. Only Aziz and Wahid were yet to find safety.

Hannah Parry

Flüchtlinge – challenging the churches/Remembering

Flüchtlinge – challenging the churches

I still remember those days in the autumn of 2015, when we first watched images of thousands of people walking across the Balkan countries, away from wars, ethnic strife and hunger. Families, single young men, unaccompanied minors …

Five years have passed since those days. Angela Merkel's call to solidarity, *'Wir schaffen das!'* ('We'll make it!'), has become a reminder that the 'refugee crisis' has not gone away. Rather, it has been pushed to the southern borders of the continent: European leaders are paying millions so that it remains there.

How to respond poses a challenge to the churches. Hospitality is theologically grounded in the affirmation that all of us are made in the image of God; and in the person of the stranger, the hungry, the sick and the outcast, we welcome Christ.

The Reformed and Roman Catholic congregations in my Zurich neighbourhood felt inspired and challenged. What does 'welcoming the stranger' mean? How could we offer these people something useful and practical in their temporary situation?

We taught German language courses; coached our students for exams necessary to enter the job market; prepared food and ate together; found babysitters to enable women to participate; collected money for a yearly excursion to the mountains.

And we have heard nearly unbelievable stories.

Sometimes we encourage people to talk about their experiences 'on the way'. One young Eritrean spoke about a boat bursting into pieces and more than one hundred people suddenly struggling in the dark waters of the Mediterranean night, screaming. 'I was praying to be spared, all of us to be spared. But I was convinced I would die. I only groaned and mumbled: "O God, O God, O God …" One of the rescue ships hurried to the spot and was able to take us in, but not all are so lucky.'

Not all want to or can talk. About leaving home. About the likelihood of never getting back, of perishing on the way. About women being afraid of being abused in the makeshift camps. About the dangers of illness or simply exhaustion.

For the past four years now I have been teaching German to refugees. One of my students was Malek, a Muslim from Syria. Shortly after he had joined the class he was diagnosed with an incurable liver disease. His only chance of survival was a transplant. When I heard this, my heart sank. He had no financial means and no health insurance. And as far as transplants are concerned, there is a list. Normally one has to wait one's turn.

The following week Malek did not show up. And nobody saw him for the next five months. Then, miraculously, the door of our classroom opened – and in came Malek, beaming with joy. He had received the transplant almost immediately – so many people had helped him to get well again. And because he was good in languages, he had a plan to study interpretation. There was hope again.

There are a thousand similar stories, little miracles which do not surface because they do not fit the political image of 'refugees', nor do they correspond easily to how the churches understand their mission. 'Yes, it includes charity work. But better not touch on issues controversial enough to lead to the loss of members.' The refugee crisis is one of those, especially when refugees raise questions about belonging, identity and rights in their new home.

The church project team had agreed that we would avoid posing as the ones who 'know', who are 'doing good'. We locals benefitted most: we learned to see ourselves through the eyes of the others. They helped us to realise how powerful the churches still are, even in Europe's secularised societies. What is needed is their presence alongside people struggling to rebuild their lives after traumatic experiences.

I have seen so many acts of kindness and respect: people understand that we are all connected. I pray with the Iona Community: *'We affirm that we are made in God's image, befriended by Christ, empowered by the Spirit.'*

I want to be part of that human family.

Remembering

I remember being a refugee myself, a little girl on the road with my family right after the war.

I was born in my mother's country, in one of those powerful old European cities: Berlin.

When I was a small child my parents had to move back to my father's country. We walked through a Europe ravaged by war, along with thousands of displaced people, all in search of a home.

Later, we lived in my father's city, another one of those famous old European places: Vienna.

After finishing my studies I moved to yet another country for work.

I married a man from another continent, full of exotic beauty.

Sometimes I did not know where I belonged.

I became a Swiss citizen, but when I speak my accent is not deemed correct. I'll never be one of them.

I found comfort in the idea that I belong to God.

Just as all other people belong to God.

Sometimes this was difficult.

Sometimes it was easy.

Over time it became easier to be different.

I asked: Why does the German word for home, or homeland, *heimat*, only exist in the singular? Can't we be at home in more than one country? And what does it mean to be human?

The best answer I received came from my son, then aged five.

I prepared him for his first day in the International School of Geneva by telling him how different his classmates would be, with a different skin colour, different languages and so on. He listened, paused and then insisted quietly, 'But they all have noses.'

Reinhild Traitler

Note: Flüchtlinge, literally 'those who are fleeing', is the German word for refugees.

At the edge of the nation

Autumn north: Iona dialogue for two voices

Voice 1:   Look to the north. The first flocks of barnacle geese and whooper swans have been seen, black and white, in the sky of Iona. They are undertaking a great sea crossing. The fast-flying geese bark to each other at the sight of landfall. The great swans of the Arctic Circle are statelier, rowing and gliding through 'glory in grey'.

Voice 2:   Look to the south. Many people are on the move: walking, burdened, waiting, fearing. Black and white, some still rich in the colours and odours of their homelands. Some carrying nothing but themselves from the utter destruction of their homes. They wait on the shore, desperate for a kindly country to give them peace and the chance of a tomorrow, but there is no rest.

Voice 1:   The Arctic skies are white and the nights freeze. We must leave now or die of cold and hunger. We must take our young and head into fierce southwesterly gales.

Voice 2:   The hot skies are red with smoke and fire, the ground parched and seeded not with crops but mines. We must leave now or die of war and hunger.

Voice 1:   Some will not survive the deep troughs of the Atlantic swell. And on our ageless path, tired and vulnerable, we are victim to poachers who know our ways and wait to shoot or net us.

Voice 2:   Lost, frightened and far from home, desperately worried about family, on the shores of the sea, we are trapped and exploited by traffickers, who pack us into unseaworthy boats.

Voice 1:   The great birds travel on from Iona, further south. They are protected by international law and a complex network of enforcement. Their wintering grounds are protected, and farmers given support to make them welcome. Their numbers are stable or increasing. Theirs is a story of peace and justice for the integrity of creation.

Voice 2:   The peoples of the south migrating to Europe are not guaranteed haven. Often, they are confined in poor accommodation, or made vagrant. Some countries have been generous, but most work hard to keep the numbers they accept to a minimum. Everywhere, generosity is countered by far-right politicians who build fences.

All: 'Lord, when did we see you hungry and feed you, or thirsty and give you something to drink? When did we see you a stranger and invite you in, or needing clothes and clothe you? When did we see you sick or in prison and go to visit you?'

The King will reply, 'Truly I tell you, whatever you did for one of the least of these brothers and sisters of mine, you did for me.'
(Matthew 25:37b–40, NIV)

Robert Walker

Volunteering in Calais, 2020

Chatting to refugees at a distribution point for an unauthorised camp in Calais was in some ways like talking to any young men. There was a lot of banter – about how many sugars they had in their coffee, where I was from in the U.K. and how many children I had. Several called me 'mummy', as I offered them biscuits, and most were younger than my own son. A game of football started with much hilarity but ended prematurely when someone kicked the ball into the nearby lake.

We distributed clothing that day as well as handing out hot drinks. There was a charging board powered by a small generator for mobile phones. Nearby we had set up a place for haircuts and beard trims. I mended some coats with large rips in them.

In other ways, talking to the refugees was different – because life is not a level playing field. They had endured persecution or were fleeing from war or conscription. They had travelled hundreds of miles with no money or shelter. They were living a precarious existence in makeshift camps, with little hope of ever returning home to their communities. We had made a choice to visit, travelling safely with our passports and credit cards in our pockets. We could sleep warmly in our beds. We could go home.

As Christians, we value every human life equally, and in Paul's letter to the Galatians we are told that *'in Christ Jesus we are all children of God: there is neither Jew nor Greek, slave nor free'*. How do we manage this in a world where there is such palpable injustice, where the accident of where and when we are born makes such a difference? How do we respond?

This is what drew me to volunteering. Firstly, we can meet this challenge by trying to attend to the experiences of displaced and marginalised people. We observe, listen, seek to break down the barriers that prevent us from hearing about life experiences which are different from our own. We work with other people of faith and good faith, seeking to bring people together into a community of care and respect. It also involves being aware of our prejudices and being open to changing our hearts and minds (much harder!).

Secondly we must align our voices with those of the powerless to challenge inequality in our world. Isaiah chapter 58 speaks of loosening the bonds of injustice and letting the oppressed go free. As Christians we aim to change hearts and minds wherever we can, to speak to those in positions of power, as well as to our friends, colleagues and communities.

Care and compassion must link with challenging power structures to help create a world where, in the words of St Paul, *'we are all one in Christ Jesus'*.

Clare Sibley

In sight of Britain

The eyes of the young stay with you. Those survivors of persecution desperate to risk the journey to a land they could see some days, and where they hope to find family, or at least a place of refuge. What do you say to a boy in his mid-teens, his eyes full of hope and hurt, with no family to back him and no future before him, trapped in a present where he is not wanted? Their stories sear the memory, however much we place protective barriers around the soul so it is not overwhelmed.

As one said, it was hard to concentrate on Covid-19 rather than death by hunger. Life in a tent, with the daily monotony of queuing for essentials, and the night-time fear of the police eviction and a run through the woods with what they can carry. The limited food and charging points, the need for shoes and more, when enduring cold, rejection, the nightmares from the journey and violence in their homeland became worse as the pandemic meant that most aid agencies pulled out. Then, on the eve of a visit by the British Home Secretary, the camps were 'cleared'. The young men living in woods around Calais were raided at dawn, forced onto buses, with no social distancing, their possessions confiscated; and were dispersed to distant parts. A few managed to remain, denied access to food, water or shelter. Some returned, shoeless, lame, thirsty. Not long afterwards, the distribution of food in Calais was banned. Charities, though harassed, continued to provide and the ban went to court.

The 'Jungle' was 'cleared' some years ago, the unaccompanied children abandoned in actions which shame us. People are still drawn to the coast, willing to risk the icy night-attempt on the Channel. Every one of those 'cleared' from the camps has a story. The terror times are not far below the surface of memory here, and sometimes the physical scars and mutilations of the journey and its captivities are on view. What answer is there when a young man washing his hands points to the sliced-off forefinger and says simply: 'Libya'? Yet we continue to return people to its shores: to rape, enslavement, extortion, death; to a society in chaos, with as many good, cowed or evil people as in our own society.

There is solidarity among refugees, even when there is no common language, faith or culture, and there is courtesy towards humanitarian workers. Even when fear, frustration and the effects of ravaged mental health are uppermost, the human spirit surprises with its generosity, the sacrificial nobility that shares out of poverty with the newcomer, that allows the man on crutches to be first in the queue. And in spite of new arrivals, the squalid conditions and the inevitable damage to refugees' physical and mental health, Covid-19 had not spread.

The stories are well-known to those who choose to inform themselves: the need to flee, the dangers of the Sahara and Mediterranean, hostility and exploitation in Europe, all that drives people here. We hear too of the faith that holds lives together.

A widowed father struggled to raise four small children in their tent: a bomb had killed his wife. A professor with a wife dying in London was one of twenty-two rescued from a capsizing dinghy, and was returned to France with hypothermia, and is desperate to try again. One teenager, after four years of trying to reach his mother in London, said: 'This is no life here. I'll risk the sea, or try to get on a lorry. I want to be a doctor.'

Another said: 'Why talk about the danger? We've crossed the Mediterranean, the Sahara. Now, some days we can see England.' A young man, with sad eyes that came alight only when he spoke of his faith, had fled Boko Haram, and now had no family to return to. 'So many died. Why am I alive?' Another sought treatment for suppurating legs caused by gunshot wounds.

Political will is needed, on an international scale. For the U.K., provision of ways to claim asylum from Calais, or from embassies, and dealing with cases swiftly, would cut the dangerous journeys, like those across the Channel; prevent criminal activity, whether people-smuggling or police brutality; cost much less, and deter purely economic migration.

Many people provide support: not all the police wished to be brutal, nor Border Guards hostile, nor local people unsympathetic. What draws people to offer support, to volunteer, other than a specific skill like medicine, a sense of duty and solidarity, and shame for their nation? (All pay their way, the hours are long, and for some the experience is overwhelming.) For a few, support is a practical expression of faith, a motivation which gained bemused acceptance by those who respected the faith met among refugees, but had otherwise viewed it as an activity for the elderly; or something brazenly presented, and rejected, as instruction and not exploration of the divine through the prism of personal experience.

The pandemic showed that a virus crosses borders in hours. With Governments astray in a world that puts profit before people, people of faith, taking our crises seriously, could show they have, after all, the will and courage to serve, speak out, and be part of the future.

Rosemary Power

God grace us

The following was conceived as a grace for the food most of us in the West, unlike our neighbours in poorer countries, managed to receive throughout the pandemic.

One volunteer with an aid organisation in northern France, after an isolated Easter, spoke of receiving a sacrificial invitation to share tea round an open fire on Eid Mubarak in a derelict warehouse in Dunkirk. As it was prepared, two young men sang a hymn of celebration, while another continued in private prayer. Shortly afterwards, the buildings, relics of the Second World War, were demolished, and the occupants forced to hide in the nearby woods, or bussed far away.

God grace us, as Sarah
and Abraham served
and sheltered the messengers
of their blessing,
that we may see your face in the exile,
we who are wanderers from Eden.

God grace us to turn from selfish hoarding,
as the rich farmer learnt that the food offered to the poor
nourished his own soul.

God grace us to share your gifts, your goods,
our time, concern and our lament,
that all may grieve and give and grow together.

When we are at home alone,
bone-weary with walking,
exhausted with serving,
chilled in a leaking tent;

isolated in grief,
angry or fearful,
numbed or shaken;

we are God's guests on earth,
and God keeps a generous table.

Rosemary Power

At the edge of society

For the child – Lord, have mercy

For the child our greed has trampled down.
Lord, have mercy.
For their blood that cries out from the ground.
Lord, have mercy.
For these lost and broken, tortured souls.
Lord, have mercy.
For those whose pain refuses to be told.
Christ, have mercy.

Lord, have mercy. Lord, have mercy.

For the nights the children cried alone.
Lord, have mercy.
For the souls that perished far from home.
Lord, have mercy.
For the child with nowhere left to hide.
Lord, have mercy.
For the silent victims of our pride.
Christ, have mercy.

Lord, have mercy. Lord, have mercy.

For our hearts that thirst for private gain.
Lord, have mercy.
For our eyes that turned and looked away.
Lord, have mercy.
For the child that 'peace' has left behind.
Lord, have mercy.

Suffering out of sight and out of mind.
Christ, have mercy.

Lord, have mercy. Lord, have mercy.

David and Rose-Mary Salmon

Dawn raid/Detention day

Dawn raid

I became involved in migration issues because I was living in a housing scheme in Scotland where a lot of people with asylum claims were placed in the local high-rise block of flats.

Crossing the park to church in my wheelchair, I smiled and greeted folk I passed, as I too was fairly new to the community. I met some of the asylum-seekers in the churches, which also ran a community centre and refugee support service.

Over time I participated in activities at the centre, and ferried folk to and from medical appointments and appointments with lawyers, and at the Border Agency offices, which were difficult to access.

I was humbled and educated as people began to share their stories, and was further shocked by how traumatic the asylum application process was. As a former social worker, I began to see for myself how negatively it affected people, especially the children.

One mother and her nine-year-old had already been detained twice when they had gone to 'sign' at the Border Agency.

This is what happened to me; and to the child:

It was 9am and I was in bed waiting for help to get up, when my new carer let them in. There were two of them, hovering over my bed. It was intimidating all the time they were there. They demanded to know where the mother and child were. I said I didn't know at present. They said I was an accessory – and could face thirteen years in prison. I told them that, the way Social Services were going, I'd be better off there: help, company, regular meals, free television …

In the end, they left, and pursued other asylum-seekers who attended the refugee centre, and even an Iona Community friend, because we'd held a prayer meeting at her house.

The mother and child finally got temporary leave to remain. That's all they still have, years later.

Over 80 members of the Community signed a letter to the Home Secretary to complain about the treatment I received. I don't know if they got an answer.

A member of the Iona Community

The child wrote this account at the age of nine:

Detention day

It's something I don't want to think about.

It's something I don't want to write about.

And it's something I don't want to hear about.

It gives me nightmares again and again. It makes me sick all the time.

[Day and date] we went to sign and we never came back home. How I wish I couldn't go to sign on that very day, if I knew something was going to happen. After signing we were told to wait because someone wanted to speak to us. My heart started racing.

We were taken to a room. When I entered I saw five or six giant men officers in blue jackets, black trousers and white shirts. They were so scary and they were staring at us. It was like we were in court and we had been found guilty of killing someone and now we were being handed to the prison guards. We were locked into the room, my whole body was numb, that's how I felt.

A woman came in reading a pile of papers.

'Your case has been dismissed. Today you are going to be detained,' she said.

Blah blah blah as she continued talking, I couldn't even listen to her, and I felt as if I was lost. I started screaming 'Please I don't want to go'. My mum too was screaming. The woman carried on reading, I kept screaming. She then offered me some tissues and a drink. I said, no thanks. The other officers were just watching us like there was a choir festival. Shortly we were locked in the van going to the *[named]* detention centre.

I was very upset. I couldn't stop thinking about my best friend ever, Fran. I was going to miss her forever. I started thinking about school. I was so excited to start primary 6 as the school holiday was about to finish. I thought of my school friends as I would miss them for a long time. I felt very upset for being disturbed from school because I knew I wouldn't be able to fulfil my dreams. How I wish I could go to high school then go to Cambridge or Oxford University, that's what I always dream about. I wished that I could change my mum's life after school. I started praying in my heart 'Please, God, help me'.

After about one hour and a half we were in *[the detention centre]*. It's a horrible place, no wonder the name sounds horrible. I felt as if I was in a different world. No friends, no good fun and no smiles from my mum. I called my friend to tell them the worst news and they screamed like someone was dead. I handed the phone to my mum to calm things. My mum too felt emotional, it was like a funeral inside the room. I had no appetite and I would only eat to fill up my stomach.

Two days later we were taken to Yarl's Wood detention centre in London. That's the worst place in my life. Many people were sad like they had lost someone in their family. I lost hope that we were going to go back to Glasgow and be back to school. There was no more happiness in my life because I felt I'd lost everything.

I never stopped praying to God. Luckily enough we met a pastor and family. We had very powerful prayers. 'God is God. Whatever is happening in life is for a purpose.'

I was sick in detention, my tonsils and my stomach were sore and I had a headache. The day I was taken to the airport I was very weak, but there was no mercy. At the last minute we were told that we were not going to fly because the flight was stopped. 'God is wonderful' I said into my heart. We went back to Yarl's Wood detention centre. The pastor and the family were glad to see us, the wife cried so bad when she saw me. We had a powerful prayer again. I prayed to God to be released so I could go back to Glasgow. I missed good food like ice cream, McDonald's and KFC.

In the morning I went to the dining hall for breakfast and an officer came to me and asked me to go with her. She told me that today we were going back home to Scotland as she took me downstairs. I told her that I also had a dream I was in Glasgow. I felt more than happy. It was a dream.

When I arrived in Scotland I couldn't wait to go and see Fran, who hugged me for a while, it was so exciting. I spent three days at that house. I said, 'I missed you a million times.' Fran's mum prepared a very nice dinner for us. The table was full of food and that was like magic. We had lots of fun together, we played in the garden, we went to the park, and when we went home we made smoothies.

Although I am out of detention I am so scared of the Home Office because it's haunting me at night. It gives me nightmares most of the time. Sometimes I jump on the bed because I dream like the Home Office is taking us to detention again, so I am trying to run away. I hate Wednesdays because it's the day I have to go and sign. The Home Office says there is no excuse, whether I like it or not I have to go to sign. I can't escape …

I feel like I'm living in the darkness, I don't know when I'm going to see the light. A million thanks to people who are helping us while we're in hard times. It's hard times for me and my mum.

Voices in a Hostile Environment

The words in this contribution are the author's own but reflect conversations with folk seeking safety in the U.K.

How can a 'Christian' country be hostile to people who mean no harm?

On my own, I left everything but I had to go.

Silence. I have no voice. I am afraid to speak. Who will speak for me? Who will speak against the angry voices?

The law aimed at organised criminals took away the little I had saved, saying it was the 'proceeds of crime'. I told the truth: that the money was mine and I had worked for it. If I had lied and said it wasn't mine, they wouldn't have taken it. What can I live on?

I fled a war zone, aged 18. I'm in my thirties now. I have a lot to offer. I could have studied. I could have learned a trade. I could have built a home and a family. I can't go back but here I have nothing and I am nothing.

Love your enemies, says Jesus. I want to be no one's enemy, yet I am rejected and despised, mocked and deprived of dignity.

Existing. Not living. Christ came to bring life in all its abundance. I want to live. I want to give. I want to love as Christ loves me and you.

Note: The term 'Hostile Environment' was first coined by Labour Immigration Minister Liam Byrne in 2007, and taken up by Conservative Home Secretary Theresa May in 2012. It described a set of measures intended to discourage people from seeking refuge in the United Kingdom by making life here demonstrably difficult for folk here 'illegally'. Although the term is no longer officially used, it still describes many of the official and unofficial attitudes to refugees and asylum-seekers in this country.

Bob Thomas

Breaking the camel's back: The hidden cost of fleeing and seeking refuge

Raped twice.
Repeatedly abused.
Tortured again.
Constantly in despair.

These are difficult words for anyone to hear or imagine. But what if these are words that describe the actual experience of you, the reader, or of someone close to you? Would you do everything you can to break the cycle and make it stop?

One of my favourite pastimes is watching children play outside with each other and with everything around them. They form bonds and connections with their environment that weave into the larger society and become memories they keep for a lifetime. Even as an adult, these bonds remain and give a man a sense of belonging and identity. Because life happens, imagine this man is suddenly or rudely uprooted and severed from the very place that always nurtured him called home. He is left with nothing, running for his life. This is the first rape, the first abuse, the first torture and the beginning of despair.

As a broken man with nothing left to lose, he picks up what pieces he can after deciding to give life another go. He reaches deep within and draws from hitherto unknown emergency reserves hoping it's enough to help him start again. He journeys long and far, only to find himself in a system that has written him off even before hearing his case. Kept endlessly on a tight leash, pushed to the very edge of his new society, told repeatedly he is lying, denied the dignity to work to pay his way, unable to study to keep himself sane, constantly threatened with deportation to a home that is no more, mental reserves all gone, eventually he snaps, killing himself or others. This second rape, abuse, torture and despair is the straw that broke the back of the camel.

Stella Olugbire

Sent to Coventry

It was December 1999 and I found myself in the back of a lorry, trying to cross the English Channel to seek sanctuary in the U.K. from the ongoing conflict in Afghanistan.

After several days in Dover, the Home Office official, with a smile, said: 'You will be sent to Coventry!' It took me some years to work out the reason for the amusement in the tone.

I knew nothing about Coventry but thanks to the warm welcome of the local community, it wasn't long before I felt like a Coventrian.

I left home in search of peace and I found myself in a city associated with peace and reconciliation. Nothing could be a better gift for someone forced to flee home in search for peace than to find welcome and hospitality in a city of peace and reconciliation.

Coventry inspired me, and especially its cathedral; both the new and old buildings have been a real source of hope for me and many others seeking protection in the city.

One sunny day I sat in the cathedral ruins looking at the new building, reflecting on how my adopted home rose from the ashes following the bombing of the city during World War II. My eyes were caught by the word 'Forgive' engraved behind the cross that was burnt during the raids. On reflection I thought forgiving is a gift from God, but only if we use it often to be more forgiving to one another and more welcoming and understanding of others' needs. This way, we can build a more welcoming and hospitable society in which people fleeing persecution and human rights violations can rebuild their lives in safety and dignity.

I now live in Glasgow, leading the Scottish Refugee Council. On a daily basis I see people arriving having endured many hardships, but with the determination to use their courage, resilience and hope to make new homes and contribute socially, culturally and economically to their adopted communities.

Sabir Zazai

Strangers and neighbours

Behind the smile

I remember walking into the classroom, sun streaming through the large windows, the patient steady smile of our lovely teacher, the women sitting donned with scarves and coats, the men nervously joking in Arabic, a couple with jaunty caps on their balding brown heads. I was here to support their English class, having survived the ordeal of my CELTA (Certificate for English Language Training for Adults) course. We had been told we were not there to be their friends or their post-traumatic counsellors. We were there to give them the gift of language: a gateway to a new life after the traumas of Syria and their long journey to the Scottish Highlands.

To start with, most did not have the language to tell us their stories, but gradually details emerged as they mimed Russian planes, stutteringly told us of the beloved roses of Aleppo, and their longing for their hometown of Homs. We noticed missing husbands and sometimes a deep silence once the smiles faded. They were always friendly: hugs from the men and smiles from the women. Always generous, often bearing gifts of baklava and other delicious goodies. They were grateful for their homes, their language classes and the support they had received from the local community. But then, usually when talking to individuals or couples, another reality appeared.

Adnan and I were sitting outside in his garden, surrounded by a forest of parsley. He was charming as always, smoking nervously on his rollup, when he told me of his news. It had been confirmed that week that his younger brother had died three years earlier in a Syrian prison. He had been taken away five years previously. I knew his father had also been taken away, but no news had been received. After taking another puff, he looked at me and said: 'It is very difficult, Simon, I know what they do to them.' He took another puff and then showed me his tomato plants.

Another student wrote:

During the war in Syria my family and I had been in a good situation because we had been living in Damascus where there was not much danger. It all started when the State Intelligence men took my father to prison. This was because a worker in his shop had put pictures mocking President Bashar on his mobile phone.

My father was released but his worker was tortured and killed. After our experience of this horror and injustice, the stories my father told us and the threats we all faced, we decided it would be better for all of us if we could get out of the country.

After two years I graduated and got engaged to Abbas, who was from Syria but living in Egypt to avoid conscription. I was happy with our marriage but not happy leaving my family in Syria. We were going to stay in Egypt but soon all of our plans changed. Five months after the birth of Ahmad, I had health problems and suddenly I lost my sight. I was diagnosed with MS. Due to my health condition and high cost of treatment, the UN provided help with our case and we were offered asylum in the U.K.

To be honest, it has been very difficult, especially for the kids. Now we are settled and starting to know how it goes here.

Mervat and Yaman were a university-educated couple. He was a lecturer in Arabic and she had done a degree in IT. They gobbled up grammar exercises without pausing for breath. They were also devout Sunnis. Yaman often sang the call to prayer in the Masjid in a rich baritone. We often discussed religion, and one day we got on to forgiveness. I trotted out some slightly trite generalisation about the Christian obligation to forgive. There was silence, and then Mervat listed the members of her family who had disappeared into the hell of a Syrian prison. 'I don't feel I need to forgive,' she said. 'I want justice. I want God's justice.' I wanted it too.

Simon Evans

You and I

I did not ask to be born into privilege.
You did not ask to be born into poverty.

We are the children of our lands,
of our communities,
of our families.

We are who we are.

But who will we be?

I have many choices.
I can share my resources
or I can keep them to myself.

I can ask questions.
I can keep silent.
I can work for justice and peace.
I can do nothing.

You have few choices:
You can be killed.
You can be persecuted.
You can flee.

You can knock on another's door
and be welcomed in
or you can be told to go away.

We are who we are.

But who will we be?

Will I care?
Will I share?

Will you survive?
Will you thrive?

Ruth Burgess

Zizzi from Zimbabwe

Positive Action in Housing (PAIH) brought Zizzi to me. She was a most attractive woman in her 30s, slim and with an upright bearing, with a charming demureness, yet she was not deferential. Quietly spoken, ready to help, she settled down and waited patiently, or so it seemed.

She had come to the U.K. for university, but after obtaining her degree had to take a basic job to provide for herself, and for her children in Zimbabwe. Her great desire was to bring them, a teenage boy and a ten-year-old girl, to Britain; she was in constant contact with them. At this time Zizzi was paying taxes and National Insurance; however, her visa expired, and because Zimbabwe was too dangerous to return to, she applied for asylum. Now she was in limbo. She could not return, neither was she allowed to stay here.

The long-drawn-out process of applying for 'leave to remain' commenced, during which she was not allowed to work: she only had vouchers for £35 a week.

A year later, she was given 'leave to remain'. She burst into my flat with the news: 'At last I can work and bring my now tall, lovely son and my mischievous, happy daughter to live with me!'

The euphoria did not last very long. She now had to find a flat, a job and ways of being united with her children, who were begging her to bring them to the U.K.

The flat she was offered was in a high-rise block. It was very dirty and had no electricity. After negotiation, the electricity was reconnected, and she returned with cleaning materials. Ready to get down on her knees to scrub the broken, splinter-laden floors, she discovered there was no water. Water restored, she began the task; but the drains were blocked, so none of the filthy water would drain away. Finally, this was rectified. Meantime she had been staying with me, along with another asylum-seeker.

Next came the job of furnishing the flat. Fortunately one of her short-term jobs had been helping at the dump, and so she had found some adequate furniture.

So with a place to stay, she continued trying to find a job. She did have several short-term ones, as a dinner lady in a school and also with a care agency.

During all this time, she had been enquiring how to bring her children here. She applied for passports for the children. However, one of the questions required the address of her place of residence, how many bedrooms this had, how much it cost, and how she would pay for it. Her present flat did not fill the requirements; so she next applied to the Council for a suitable house. However this application form required the passport numbers of the children. No passport numbers – no house. No house – no passport numbers.

We filled in the passport application form with the details of my flat, which met the requirements. A small amount of rent did change hands, as the form required her to already have possession of the flat for the children's arrival.

To do this she worked extremely long and hard hours with a care agency, spending almost nothing on herself. Friends and relatives also came to her aid with some money.

In November 2010, Zizzi's children arrived in Glasgow. Now the girl goes to school – a happy, bubbly child. Her brother, tall, slim and handsome, hopes to do a college course on nutrition. He had passed his A-level exams in Zimbabwe.

Soon after they arrived I asked them if they would like to join the youth group at our church. 'Oh, yes please,' they replied. The boy has also joined a small amateur theatre group and has already appeared on stage.

A good ending to this story, and I hope it remains so. Unfortunately, their mum could only find work in England, so the son and his sister stay together in Glasgow.

Sally Beaumont

We get a glimpse

We get a glimpse of panic
but still we cling to what we know.
Some get more than a glimpse – it's all we can do to keep going;
the worries of others are beyond our coping.
Still we must try.

How much imagination do we need?
How much panic before we begin to see
there really is a different way?
Too much it seems.
Horror at the images on our screens.
Too much, so we switch off.
Someone should do something.
But not us, or if us then only a bit.
Because, after all, it is not our fault.

Who is my neighbour?
Yes, the folk next door.
Yes, family and friends.
The stranger? The enemy? Yes,
yes, and yes again.
Most friends were once strangers.
Many allies were once enemies.
Love is the only way.

Imagine yourself in an overcrowded boat.
Imagine your son or daughter – young or old –
hiding in a refrigerated truck, or clinging to the axle.
Imagine your friends, your parents, your colleagues,
facing challenges you wouldn't wish on your worst enemy.
May your worst imaginings never happen to you or them.
May your worst imaginings galvanise you
to care for those to whom it is happening now,
to welcome those who need welcome.

Give what you can, give up what you can.
And then some more.
Be the widow giving her mite.
Be the butterfly beating its wings.
Be the one who dares to march to the beat of a different drum.
Be the drop in the ocean.
Be the straw which tips the system into changing.
Be the cliché which makes a difference.
'Be the change you want to see.'

Help bend the arc of the moral universe towards justice.
That arc may be long
but together we can bend it more quickly.

Liz Gibson

Meeting Christ over tahini

'Often goes the Christ in the stranger's guise.'
From an Iona prayer of hospitality

A few years ago, I worked at a night shelter for destitute asylum-seekers and refugees in our church. This was in partnership with the Manchester-based charity Boaz Trust.

Our purpose was simple: to serve our visitors' practical needs by providing food, a warm shower and a safe place to sleep. But they were not content to passively receive our help: many would ask us to sit and eat with them. They wanted to learn about us, and to be known and recognised as fellow people with names, stories and histories.

Once, over supper, one man grabbed a jar of tahini dressing and held it up, saying almost through tears, 'Ever since I came to the U.K. a few years ago, I have not eaten tahini. Eating this now brings me right back to my family.' He was from Saudi Arabia, and I remember him most for his keen sense of humour despite his tragic circumstances. When he found out that I was married but that we didn't have children yet, he commanded me to name our first son after him.

Most of the men were Muslims, and we got used to their dietary requirements for halal meat. One man from northern Africa, however, was unusual: for several weeks he didn't eat meat, dairy or eggs, nor did he eat anything before 3pm. He was an Orthodox Christian, fasting to observe the season of Advent, a practice I hadn't heard of before. Through meeting the men, I learned not only about other faiths, but also more about my own Christian faith.

It was humbling to encounter these men who, every day, relied upon the care of others. Often, while returning home from the night shelter, I would feel a mixture of things – a sense of unfairness, but also that my own humanity had somehow been deepened through my interactions with them.

Jesus says that whenever we welcome a stranger, we welcome Jesus himself (Matthew 25:34–40). Although we didn't recognise it at the time, I believe that in meeting and serving our guests, we were spending time with Christ. The men often thanked us and praised God for the food, shelter and friendship we offered, but I too must give thanks and praise to God for the blessings I received from them.

Josh Seligman

At the heart of humanity

I had just finished my talk on refugees when she rushed up to me.

'My son is at school with a child who has fled from Syria. I would like to help.'

'Great!' I said. 'We need English teachers, befrienders and people like you to spread the word that we need houses for families to come to the U.K. and live in.'

So she bought a house, and a family of five came.

I went through the checklist:

House – check.
Beds – check.
Refrigerator – check.
Cooker – check.
Toys – check …

The list went on and people gave.

I approached the young white neighbour. She held her infant close when I told her of her new neighbours arriving next week.

A few months passed.

I was at work, helping customers in a shop. A young family waited. They smiled and gestured for my attention when I had finished. I did not at first recognise them when they smiled and said *'As-salamu alaykum'*.

'We love our neighbours!' they announced to everyone within earshot. 'We have learned so much! We share meals and recipes. The children walk our dog with us. We are learning Arabic as fast as we can. We wish we knew more.'

My eyes welled up.

Penny Gardner

The knowledge that empowers

Migrants and refugees as social entrepreneurs

I've been working with people from refugee and other migrant backgrounds for a number of years now. Like many others, I started by offering help to folk in obvious need, particularly asylum-seekers affected by the horrible U.K. asylum system and by Fortress Europe's murderous borders. As I spent longer with refugees and other migrants, however, the relationship developed and I discovered that my specific skills as an accountant and charity administrator could be very useful.

I joined the boards of Right to Remain and Positive Action in Housing, organisations set up by British activists for racial and migration justice, but with a number of migrants on their Management Committees.

One friend wanted to set up a charity to support humanitarian relief in his country of origin. He had all the skills, and some good support, but just needed a little help from me in drafting a constitution that would enable him to register the charity and open a bank account. His group has been running successfully for almost ten years now.

Another friend had set up, and run successfully for a number of years, an arts charity connecting up African diaspora artists and practitioners from across Scotland. Here the lack was in the area of bookkeeping skills, and all that was needed was some sorting out of bank statements to keep the organisation compliant and able to keep running.

More recently, I gave advice on charitable fundraising rules to a group of young people from various regional backgrounds who were organising a fundraising concert for Yemen. In this case, none of them was from Yemen itself but their experience of war-torn countries made them want to help what seems to be a much-neglected cause. The concert was a great success and funds have been sent.

Without even giving advice I have been a beneficiary of wonderful cultural events, concerts, ceilidhs and performances from organisations set up and largely run by people from refugee and other migrant backgrounds, now enriching the general cultural scene in Glasgow and beyond.

There are so many other examples of initiatives and organisations set up by people from refugee and other migrant backgrounds. Understandably many of these focus on the needs experienced by these folk themselves, both humanitarian and cultural, but many others spread their benefits far wider. I am so grateful for the energy, skill and commitment of people who are making Scotland and the U.K. their home, and for the vibrancy and strength that this is giving to our social and cultural life.

Robert Swinfen

Environmental factors in the movement of people

In August 2020, BBC News covered a story from Kenya reporting that flooding caused by months of heavy rain had led to thousands of people being forced from their homes. Two large lakes were so close to combining, there were worries they would contaminate each other, thus polluting the freshwater source for the surrounding areas.[1]

On the low-lying islands of Kiribati in the central Pacific Ocean, warming temperatures, increasing rainfall and rising sea levels are endangering the lives and livelihoods of the population of 110,000. Coastlines are eroding, freshwater supplies are at risk from the higher tides, which drown the wells in salt water, and fish supplies, a core part of the islanders' diet, are failing, as the coral reefs that feed the fish can't survive in the warming waters. Predictions are that, by the year 2100, sea levels will make half of the islands unlivable. The government is planning for a mass migration of the population; one that *'preserves the dignity of those being relocated and mini- mises the burden on the receiving countries'*, according to the Office of the President.[2]

Increasingly, climate change impacts on the world's poorest and most vulnerable people, who are the least responsible for its causes. In 2019 Oxfam noted that over the last ten years climate disasters were the major factor driving internal displacement, *'forcing more than 20 million people a year ... to leave their homes'*.[3] People who are already living in extreme poverty have no reserves to fall back on when climate change factors hit; these include crop-rust on coffee plants in Guatemala, drought in Ethiopia and desertification in central China.[4]

Climate change and environmental destruction are significant factors in conflicts. In Syria, a prolonged drought led to a mass migration from rural areas into urban centres. The resulting demographic change and impact on increasingly scarce resources significantly exacerbated an already tense political situation. For many individuals and families in such circumstances, external migration becomes the only choice.[5]

> *'There has been a tragic rise in the number of migrants seeking to flee from the growing poverty caused by environmental degradation. They are not recognised by international conventions as refugees; they bear the loss of the lives they have left behind, without enjoying any legal protection whatsoever.'* (Pope Francis, in *Laudato Si'*, 2015)[6]

For many refugees arriving on our shores, the trauma of the journey to get here is only a part of it – many have not only lost their homes and families, but a way of living and the connection to the land that they knew and the stories that they told.

In Europe, loss of biodiversity and extreme weather events are becoming increasingly common occurrences. How might our growing climate-change awareness help us to better hear other people's stories, and to really understand what our refugee brothers and sisters have lost? How might our care for them help us in our efforts to be better stewards of God's glorious creation of which we're all a part?

Action points:

- *Learn* about the links between climate change and refugees. The UNHCR website is a good place to start, and many environmental and faith organisations also have good, up-to-date information.

- *Listen* to refugees and asylum-seekers in your community; building friendships and fellowship is a central part of helping refugees to integrate and feel welcome.

- *Campaign* for better support for refugees and policies that respect the dignity of all.

- *Pray* for all those affected by climate change across the world, and for our ability to change our behaviour.

Miriam McHardy

Notes:

1. 'Rising water levels in Kenya's Great Rift Valley threaten jobs and wild-life,' BBC News, 16th August, 2020, video by Joe Inwood and Ferdinand Omondi:

www.bbc.co.uk/news/av/world-africa-53776774

2. CMSOnAir|Pelenise Alofa on Climate Change Migration, Center for Migration Studies:

https://cmsny.org/multimedia/cmsonair-pelenise-alofa

'Health and climate change: country profile 2017: Kiribati', World Health Organisation, 3rd December, 2018:

www.who.int/publications/i/item/health-and-climate-change-country-profile-2017-kiribati

3. 'Climate-fuelled disasters number one driver of internal displacement globally, forcing more that 20 million people a year from their homes', Anna Ratcliff, Oxfam, 2nd December, 2019:

www.oxfam.org/en/press-releases/forced-from-home-eng

4. 'As climate effects hit coffee crops, Guatemalan farmers become migrants', Sarah Salvadore, Earthbeat, 20th September, 2019:

www.ncronline.org/news/earthbeat/climate-effects-hit-coffee-crops-guatemalan-farmers-become-migrants

'Unpacking climate change and the Horn of Africa crisis', Alex Randall, Climate and Migration Coalition:

https://climatemigration.org.uk/climate-change-horn-africa-crisis

'Halting the desert', 9th November, 2018, UNA-UK:

www.climate2020.org.uk/halting-the-desert

5. 'Climate change in the Fertile Crescent and implications of the recent Syrian drought', Colin P. Kelley, Shahrzad Mohtadi, Mark A. Cane, Richard

Seager and Yochanan Kushnir, Proceedings of the National Academy of Sciences of the United States of America, 17th March, 2015:

www.pnas.org/content/112/11/3241

6. Encyclical Letter *Laudato Si'* of the Holy Father Francis on Care for our common home, 2015:

www.vatican.va/content/francesco/en/encyclicals/documents/ papa-francesco_20150524_enciclica-laudato-si.html

Blessing

Beannachadh/Blessing

Is clachan beò sinn,
air ar coisrigte don Tighearna.
Rachamaid a-nis,
togamaid, nar coimhearsnachdan agus nar beathanan, taigh ùr.
Togamaid taigh ùr, far an cluinnear mac-talla fuaim a mholaidh
am measg nan clach beò,
agus far am bi fàilte agus fasgadh don fhògarrach,
bòrd agus aran do gach aon air a bheil acras,
agus làmhan fosgailte gus ar creideamh a chur an gnìomh.
Amen.

We are living stones,
consecrated to the Lord.
Let us go now,
and let us build, in our communities and in our lives, a new house.
Let us build a new house, where the living stones will resound
with the sound of his praise
and where there will be welcome and shelter for the exile,
table and bread to all who hunger,
and open hands to put our faith into practice.
Amen.

Donnchadh Sneddon/Duncan Sneddon

Some websites

Boaz Trust: www.boaztrust.org.uk

Care4Calais: https://care4calais.org

Choose Love/Help Refugees: https://helprefugees.org

FCEI–Mediterranean Hope: www.mediterraneanhope.com

Friends without Borders: www.friendswithoutborders.org.uk

No Name Kitchen: www.nonamekitchen.org

Positive Action in Housing: www.paih.org

Refugees at Home: www.refugeesathome.org

Refugee Council: https://refugeecouncil.org.uk

Right to Remain: https://righttoremain.org.uk

Scottish Refugee Council: www.scottishrefugeecouncil.org.uk

Sherborne Area Refugee Support (SHARES):
www.sherbornearearefugeesupport.org.uk

Third Hope: http://thirdhope.org

Sources and acknowledgements

Holy Bible, New International Version®, NIV® Copyright ©1973, 1978, 1984, 2011 by Biblica, Inc.® Used by permission. All rights reserved world-wide.

'You'll die at sea', by Abdel Wahab Yousif, from the Care4Calais Facebook page and website. Used by permission of Care4Calais.

The writers

Laila Khaled Alrefai became a refugee from Syria in her mid-teens, with her family scattered. She is now in her late twenties, married with children and living in the U.K.

Sally Beaumont is a member of the Iona Community, now in her 80s, who, for many years, has opened up her home to provide hospitality to asylum-seekers.

Ruth Burgess is a member of the Iona Community, living in Dunblane. She enjoys being retired, growing fruit, flowers and vegetables, writing and editing, and paddling along the shoreline whenever she gets a chance.

Margaret Connor (1930-2014) was a poet, fabric artist and teacher, who spent her childhood in the Caribbean and most of her adult life in the Moravian Settlement at Fulneck in Yorkshire. This poem is reproduced with the consent of her family.

Elizabeth Davison was craftworker on Iona in 2014 and 2015. She is a retired educator who works at making art and writing.

Simon Evans is a retired Consultant Chest Physician, who has recently returned to work after obtaining his CELTA. For the last two years he has worked with Syrian refugees in the Scottish Highlands. He is a member of the Iona Community.

Penny Gardner is an Iona associate who, as part of Sherborne Area Refugee Support (SHARES), has been actively supporting the resettlement of refugees in Dorset.

Liz Gibson is a member of the Iona Community and an organic crofter and minister living on Mull with her husband, Martyn.

Charles Hulin teaches music theory and composition at a Christian college in Lakeland, Florida. He is a pianist and the composer of the faith-integrating piano curriculum, *Pilgrimage of Practice*, based on stories of St Columba.

Fiona Kendall is European and Legal Affairs Advisor for FCEI-Mediterranean Hope, a project supporting migrants in Italy. She is an Iona Community associate.

Rory MacLeod has spent time in both the army and navy, and with the Gulf Peace Team in Jordan and Israel. He is a Church of Scotland minister, currently in Skye, and writes in both Gaelic and English.

Miriam McHardy is a writer and spiritual director, with a particular passion for encouraging the connections between faith, justice and the environment. She lives in East Lothian with her family where she is a member of her local Catholic parish, a growing eco-congregation.

Godfrey Meynell is a Christian poet from Derbyshire, an Arabic speaker and an environmentalist. Now long retired, he and his family are engaged in climate-change action, organic farming and refugee support.

Stella Olugbire is happy for the opportunity to heal and rebuild her life in Scotland as a refugee. She wants to retrain as a mental health specialist in order to better support others like herself.

Hannah Parry is a church organist and professional scuba diver who has been volunteering with aid organisations helping people on the move in France and the Balkans, often providing first aid. Find out more at www.hannahparry.co.uk

Neil Paynter is an editor, writer and late-night piano player. Previously he worked as an ESL teacher, and in nursing homes and homeless shelters. He is an associate of the Iona Community.

Rosemary Power is a writer and member of the Iona Community, who has worked in a range of church ministries, and as a voluntary sector worker, shepherd and academic. She spent several weeks volunteering in the unsanctioned refugee camps of northern France.

David and Rose-Mary Salmon are the founders of Third Hope Africa, a charity working in northern Uganda for the recovery of ex-child soldiers abducted as children and forced to commit atrocities during the long civil war, and who are now engaged in the long and painful process of reintegration into the community. They wrote 'For the child – Lord, have mercy' to remember their stories, and to stand with the displaced children of our world.

Josh Seligman's work among refugees includes coordinating a church night shelter, teaching English in Manchester and tutoring primary-school students in California. He has been a staff member of the Iona Community on Iona, and now works as a freelance proofreader and editor. In his spare time he edits *Foreshadow*, an online Christian literary magazine. He lives in Cumbria with his wife.

Clare Sibley is a new member of the Iona Community and currently working as part of the resident staff on Iona. She volunteered with Care4Calais in February 2020, and is a home visitor for Refugees at Home, meeting prospective hosts for refugees trying to settle in the U.K.

Donnchadh/Duncan Sneddon was born in Scotland and grew up in Pakistan in a missionary family. He currently works as a research assistant in Celtic and Scottish Studies at the University of Edinburgh and is an occasional preacher at the Gaelic services at Greyfriars Kirk in Edinburgh and for Eaglais Air-loidhne Ghàidhlig.

Robert Swinfen is a previous Support Services Manager of the Iona Community. He now works as Finance Director of SCIAF (Scottish Catholic International Aid Fund). He has been a member of the Iona Community since 2003.

Bob Thomas is a member of the Iona Community, a retired teacher and volunteer for 'Friends without Borders', a charity supporting refugees and asylum-seekers in Portsmouth.

Reinhild Traitler, educator and theologian, worked with the World Council of Churches, and later was Director of the Boldern Protestant Academy, Zurich. She is a member of the Swiss Interreligious Think Tank, co-founder of the European Project for Interreligious Learning (EPIL), the author of several books, a grandmother and a member of the Iona Community.

Robert Walker is an associate of the Iona Community, who worked on Iona as Maintenance Coordinator for two years. His interests in botany and ornithology join together in a love of Iona's natural history.

Abdel Wahab Yousif (1990-2020) was well known among young poets in Sudan. Despite his upbringing in poverty he obtained a degree at the University of Khartoum, but had to flee his home in desperate search of safety. It has proved impossible to obtain formal permission to publish this poem, but it is printed here to honour Abdel, and all who die seeking safety.

Sabir Zazai is Chief Executive Officer of the Scottish Refugee Council, and was previously CEO of Coventry Refugee and Migrant Centre. The war in Afghanistan meant that he was internally displaced with his family when he was still in primary education, but he has since achieved post-graduate qualifications, and an Honorary doctorate for his human rights work.